MONEY
LAUNDERING

Also written by the Poet

HOW TO FALL IN LOVE: A BEGINNER'S BIBLE

MONEY
LAUNDERING

A Whistleblower Story

Oluebube

Ogbonnaya

ISBN: 979-860-04336-2-5

This is for my fathers
Ogbonnaya and Chikaodiri

I have two problems with Money Laundering
One. Elites move money meant for the Poor in a settlement
   To another settlement
Two. Three Poor children die at the announcement
   Of every successful Money Laundering

My Dear Governor, Senator and President
I believe you're Saint
Thus this story isn't about you.

And please don't act
Like you've lost to self-guilt
I completely trust you

MONEY LAUNDERING

This is for my father
This is for my mother
This is for my eternal-year-old brother

"This is for the entire state
This is for us all, we the children of fate
This is for us all, that choose not to hate

We've come this far
We've seen our state jaws ajar
But today, we've chosen to wish on a star

A lot has happened
A lot less has changed
A lot has been wasted

By our so-known big men
By our clueless congressmen
By those bundle of an excuse of statesmen

That rose to power with our blood
That boycott our democratic belief and code
That choose to fulfil not their word

That choose to treat us with heavenly wickedness
That see the state as a family business
That takes for granted our meekness

But, I assure you something
I, Dr Baba will be as humble as nothing
I will decrease that we might increase in everything

I will not
I will never fight
I will never fight against our collective interest

I will be the best you've seen
I will take us to heights we've never been
I will see even the least of us as a human being

We'll conquer our fears
We'll be ahead of our peers
We'll be ahead of other states by nine years

We'll jealously guard our blood sweat and tears
We'll uplift the vision of our heroes and pioneers
We'll retire embezzlement, making sure it disappears

For good
For today and together we've withstood
Them all, for good

I'm here for us all
I'm erecting my office in the town hall
I'm going to be accountable for us all

God transform our democratic fate
God bless our state
God bless Kaivu State."

"Doc, you've restored our pioneers' political scope
You've restored the people's hope
With restored hope, they'll cope

I'm glad to be an accomplice of yours
To be with you behind closed doors
To be beside you as you settle scores

We have spent years perfecting our stores
We have tightened our borders and shores
We will give the state as many coiffures

At the end of our stay here, we'll bag honours
We'll leave the statehouse with underscores
Only then, shall we rest on our oars."

Tell me what I'll accomplish without Tella
I'll accomplish not a thing. She's my propeller
Without her, I won't have stood this taller

—

I am a believer
I have grown to empathize it's a stance so clever
I am also, to a degree, a non-believer

I looked around the church and
I see people devotedly stupid
I see a congregation squarely impoverished

I see rags seated
I see souls spiritual and captivated
I see the cheater seating next to the cheated

That sent tears strolling down my cheeks
That told me the church has weak checks and balances
That wasn't the best of experience

For a newly elected Governor like me
For a systematic Messiah like me
For a soul that doesn't fit to a T.

I could have fitted to their T
But tragedy is their T

Transgression is their T

I believe in shared prosperity
I work two four seven for a happier posterity
I represent discipline and integrity

With minor compromise of sincerity
Judge me not. I made love with severity
Not once not twice. That gave birth to our disparity

Here the more money you give the more you get
The more prayer dosage you get
Here the poor get a cold sweat

Here the rich wring wet
From the joy they get seeing the poor fret
And tremble at their feet

Jesus will be ashamed of this invention
That's if he loves the rest of us his creation
Those of us still stuck crying for redemption

In Kaivu, million-dollar chapel's a reality
Feverish looking school's a reality
Life-threatening hospital's a reality

Clergies being guarded by an army's a reality
Clergies being treated abroad's a reality
Members drinking water for treatment's a reality

Members wearing aprons for security
Members afflicted with financial insecurity
Members in need of new mindsets is a reality

By the way, patronize me. I sell mindsets
London fairly used mindsets
And brand new mindsets

"Challenge God." that's the man of God
Calling for donations for his all mighty God

God's grace explains my inaugural mood

I'll challenge his God
Not because he asked
But because I wanted

"Three million Dollars."
"Child of God bow and receive God's blessings.
Success will envelope all your deeds."

I've gotten all I needed. So, to my feet, I rose.
Success will envelope all my deeds
Seriously, All. My. Deeds.

Tella gives wonderful advice
She talked me into God's presence
Now, look what I've got as proceeds

With an All Mighty's protection, I am unstoppable
I will do the undoable
I will pieces diamonds with my ankle.

I'll make Kaivu Desert arable
I'll set amidst my opponents a glass table
I'll render principalities in high places broke and unstable

—

It's my day one as Governor
I need to look my best, not better
I need to be charming and sexier

Not to get approved by others
Their approval's irrelevant, here I give the orders
Seeking their approval shows gross disorders

It's me to command respect
Not beg for it
That's a Dr Baba fact.

Be careful
A need my eyes handful
Today's the Alpha of a tenure insane and wonderful

"Sweethearts, don't worry I'll proceed, myself."
"Doc, are sure you want to do this yourself."
"Tella, Chief loves it when I do it myself."

I haven't done my makeup in two years
I was busy facing my fears
Brazing my gears

Briefing volunteers
Meeting with financiers
Leaping towards drying my tears

With the first phase complete
It's in place for a treat
I'll treat myself with a makeup neat and elite

My face has already been moistened
And my fake lashes fixed
So, I introduced

The face primer and the foundation
With utmost attention
Get it wrong, and I see a million adulation

And look like some coat of many colours
Our mother made for us.
My concealer and the naughty blemishes

Fought for a while. And a winner
Of course, my concealer
Emerged — she's a fighter

Wake the face with a highlighter. Check
In-depth contouring. Check
Brush the cheeks apple. Check

Primer, eyeshadow, liner. Check
Looked forward and applied a stroke
Upward with a mascara. Now I'm awake

I can't help but steal couple glances
Of myself. Wow, I see new acquaintances
I see credible alliances

Lip sealer. Check
Lip liner. Check
Then, my signature Copper Brown lipstick

"Volume please."
"It's nine and her Excellency is not in the office
She's clueless."

"I need to be on that Television, in minutes."
The studio isn't far from my residence
So in minutes, we were there ourselves

Power's sweet, the security didn't
Lay a finger on me. I enter the set
And hugged and kissed the cheat

He's Chief Dan, my predecessor and opponent
I stole his second term. It's more polite
Than saying, "I sponsored his defeat."

"Baby Dan, who wouldn't be clueless.
You promised to drive me to the State House
I've been calling since six

Don't tell me that excuse
Of a wife, I mean your mistress
Stopped you again. Baby, please

I'm going nowhere without you. Yes
Less I forget, come over to the house
Say seven or six

My husband isn't home tonight
So maybe we can do away with this fight
The power fight. I miss our pillow fight

And come prepared
I would love a couple of rounds
I wouldn't like you limp on the second or third

Take care, see you tonight."
And I left him searching for his feet
"Ignore her, she is an ailment..."

Why is loss or defeat
So difficult
A reality to accept

His Man of God probably sent
Him a "You'll be the first
And not the last."

Prophetic message.
I'm not surprised, at his age
He oughts to opt for a head massage

More often.
Like serious, I mean
Every word I'm saying.

"Unleash the dogs, Tella."
And she followed my command to the latter
Unleashing a herd of calm journalists. Later

We heard they exchanged sixteen punches
They exchanged harsh words
And worst, complimentary cards

—

Our school system's one of the best

Teachers well equipped
Students possessed

By some Shakespearean spirit
Possessed by Adam Smith
And even by inventors like Wright

Kaivu students are extremely brilliant
Thus, they're always at home to invest
More in entrepreneurship — hawking in the street

They are the bravest
They are the most progressed
They work in the state's interest

Regardless of the fact that each day
A child gets to leave his dream Midway
A child is opportune to paint the highway

With his goods, and
With his sweat and blood
This is a Kaivu story. Blunt and Bold

As for the national exam council
Internationally known for habitual
Mass failures, cancel

Exam results
They encourage mass resits
They reward students

Students who cheat
Who cheat to escape resit
Because resit once and it becomes a habit

Kaivu boasts of European standard classrooms
European standard of the World Wars
A teenage teacher per hundred pupils

There shall be showers of blessing
There's no better way of expressing
What pupils see during raining

Seasons. With leaking roofs
Zero doors
Patched windows

The singing of God's promises keeps them warm
Keeps them alive and uniform
That they may live to see another academic term

In a time where European pupils
Bring internet-enabled tablets
To schools

It's a crime punishable by expulsion
To bring cell phones to a school in session.
Kaivu is synonymous to academic depression

But, that narrative, my tenure must kill
The gaps I'll fill
And every Kaivu student will

Be glad I seized power
Will christen my tenure, Liberation Hour
And me, that woman with seven-man willpower.

I'm a doer
I'm not a moaner
I'm not the type that lives in an Ivory Tower

Suffering and smiling explains the Ivory Tower
It's akin to being a backbencher
It's akin to lack of willpower

"Previous administrations celebrate
This fraudulent system, but not
Anymore. This time, we'll fight

We'll emasculate
We'll dehydrate
We'll annihilate

Every ill in our education system
For a depressed doom
Awaits states clueless with her education system

Kaivu students, this day I give you free education
Every educational facility will gain internet connection
This isn't just a proclamation

We'll break ground this minute
No dull moment
Dull–moment–phobia is right and just."

Every millisecond of our day one made headlines
Audacious headlines
Courtesy of our press corps — the dogs

—

We lived the moment
To the fullest
And aside education, we touched Health

I'll call a spade, a spade
And a shovel, a shovel. God forbid
That I lay things on the thick. I'd

Never be happy to have you deceived
Dear, being treated
In Kaivu in lieu of going abroad

Is the third most risky activity in the world
It's riskier than being religious in North Korea, and
Worse than base jumping would

Ever be. It's life-threatening
From facilities visibly decaying

To practitioners whose orientations' derailing

Hospitals lack of hospitality
Is an abnormality
To behold. It lacks geniality and spirituality

Ops. I think there's an atom of spirituality
In them. But not a presence of geniality
Which ought to have been a normality

It's rare to see doctors
In Kaivu hospitals
All we see are music lovers

Loitering medical facilities
With medical earphones
Around their necks or in their hands

Worst is the sight of butchers
In medical suits
They love damning consequences

Every week, wombs are damaged
Test tubes mismatched
And hospital gates closed

For three days straight
For one week straight
For one to three months straight

Because the practitioners are unpaid
Because the practitioners are underpaid
Because the governments are afraid

To give the masses a good life
For good life translates to strife
And strife begets indifference towards the afterlife

For long afterlife have been in the First eleven
Courses for being a backbencher. Even

The educated would choose to not get even

With leaders who've chosen
To see them as a burden
To feed them to pets in their dungeon

These excuse of leaders invest in dungeons
They can surrender pensions
Just to get demons for their dungeons

Poverty constitutes the majority of the demons
With hunger, unemployment amongst others.
Why get even with oppressors

When afterlife has made promises
Promises of happiness
In some undemocratic paradise

A healthy nation is a wealthy nation
A wealthy nation is a developed nation
And In a developed nation

Cluess leaders like ours face stiff opposition
Kaivu leaders despise opposition
Thus, they'll invoke massive oppression

You'll nevermind these ills until
You encounter them eyeball to eyeball
Until oppression pushes you downhill

With her contacts.
Her contacts constitute principalities
In high places

And those of us
In low places –
Those of us praying for unmerited favours.

Those of us with our hands in the till
Those of us that can't foot our bill

That don't want these oppressors over the hill

I've seen our ill-health departments manifest
I've seen lives walk away after an accident
Not due to the accident's fatality, but

Because our health institutions had her gate
Closed, due to unpaid this and that
I've seen governable circumstances separate

The body from its soul and spirit
I've seen lives swept under the carpet
Especially children who ought to be our ticket

To prosperity
To continuity
To longevity

But, from this day
We'll improve our institutions every day
From this day

We'll lead happier lives
Regardless of economic divides
Regardless of religious divides

And it came to pass
On our first day in office
We launched a series of health initiatives

One thing about our day one in office
We damned several consequences
I'll tell you about the consequences

...
My dear, it's that grave
But, our administration's brave

We'll face them all

Even if they will
Raise an army from the pit of hell

—

"Dr Baba's becoming a political superwoman
In less than forty-eight hours of an
Administration

She has put the state in
Jeopardy, and to worsen
Matters she's dragging every soul in

This room down.
Down to earth, where none
Of us would ever dream of being

She has withdrawn
The state from the National Education
Certificate Examination

She has given
Free buses to commute Men
Women and Children

She has converted an
Entire state into a free trade zone
More than a million

Medicines have been
Allotted to village clinics. To worsen
These, is to let her continue her season

Of change
Trust me, this strange
Woman will derange

All of us in no distant
Time. Trust me this and that

We've seen is but

A supporting film. The worst
Of agenda is yet
To sprout."

I knew something was fishy. This morning
I got a tip about a caucus happening
Beneath my nose. Every gathering

Not in my favour invariably is demanding
My wrath. I barge into the gathering
"Prof. Badmus, you are cuddling

With the devil's favourite demon. Outstanding
Of you to join these cheats, notwithstanding
All we've being ..."

Prof. Badmus is my deputy
And today, he's chairing a committee
Or better STill, a coup. What enormity.

By the way, the first
Day I paid him a visit
It took me a lot

To figure him out
In his living room. On a serious note
He's all over the room, with

Fifteen portraits of him on the wall
Six of which's five feet tall
Identifying the real

Prof. Badmus isn't easy
And one could get queasy
By just sitting here daily

—

It's human to plan a coup. I'll leave you guys
To continue your caucus
But. One thing's

Certain, you are all messing with
The Devil's favourite demon. Just
Pray I don't leave this hut

With my body, soul and spirit intact
Else, you all will regret
Showing interest

In my downfall. Thanks all
If you need assistance don't hesitate to call
That reminds me, can I get a glass or a bottle."

It's me to gulp some alcohol
Whenever I'm tensed. A little
Sip and I'm okay and agile

I picked a bottle
Of whiskey from their table
Its content ran down the aisle

Of my stomach like a group of little
Men, and then rode up the aisle
With a bicycle

Be careful. Girl. Be careful
I felt the cable
That runs down my bowel

Getting full
And worst, I felt not so slight abdominal
Pain. Now my mouth's full

With whatever that drove up the cable
Or the aisle. Now I fell
Fragile

I tried to run as far from them as possible
But, before I could leave them all
I emptied my bowel

What was in that bottle
It couldn't have been a regular alcohol
I can take two bottles of whiskey and still

Be as still as water. "Prof. Badmus!"
And six of him came, "Prof. Badmus
What was in that bottle? Tell me please..."

"Phase two complete."
What's he talking about ...
And I saw Abraham, Isaac and Jacob with

Their friend Adam Smith
Drinking from two empty bottles at
Some apparent local restaurant

—

My ears woke to voices in the street
I heard hawkers sell their market
I heard cars blare from a distance, "At last,

Doctor, Dr Baba's awake."
And my eyes woke
"Tella, please give me a break

It's not like I slept the whole week —
Who sleeps for a whole week."
"Doc. You've been asleep since last week

I found you helpless and weak
That should be Tuesday last week
Thank goodness, you're awake."

I tried leaving the bed
But was restricted

By a cuff. Was I arrested?

Tella hands me my phone
Apparently, Chief Dan's been
Calling my private line

"Baby, I know you haven't heard
Plans are been perfected
So soon you will not need

To perambulate my state doing good
And yes, we've successfully arrested
You. And by four today you'll be imprisoned

For bypassing legislative processes
Illegal procurement of public funds
Electoral Malpractices

Embezzlement of public funds
Treasonable Felony amongst others
A total of fifty-three count charges

It's noteworthy that you'll spend
Or remain imprisoned
For the next sixteen years and

Also, you'll pay a fine totalled
One billion dollars. Don't misunderstand
Me, you'll pay the fine and also be imprisoned

You could
Have just died
You know, you were poisoned

Not by some spirit
We all at the caucus did it
You know the shocking side it

We worked with your allies
Give me a shocked face

I love getting faces.

Tella tipped us
Bye, let me leave you with your worries."
"Please, don't do this

I'll make amends I promise
I'll give it to you whichever stance
You prefer. I promise."

"I hate it when you talk to me about sex
Young woman, I have a lot of toys
I even export women overseas

See you in court
Less I forget
Once you're impeached

I'll regain my seat
Your deputy will shift
He's not a potential opponent

Because we'll throw him off the cliff
He's as weak as a handkerchief
Not even the Calif or the Pontiff

Will fortify him to match my strength
I wish you the very best
Sweetheart

Less I forget, Tella can I see your face
This once
You made the right choice."

I must be dead or something
Of all my allies. He's lying
Tella can't betray me. Chief's lying

"Doc, I'm sorry."

And I took a selfie
Hashtag Unhappy

—

Three Thirty prompt
I arrived at the court
I was weak but on the sight

Of my Kaivu faithfuls, my weakness burned
I felt possessed
By Nelson Mandela. I regained

My voice my passion
My mission my vision
And my sense of fashion

I looked myself in the mirror
I couldn't see a moaner
All I saw was a doer

Jesus said to me "Success
Will envelope all your deeds."
Just about to address my faithfuls

Chief Dan joined
"Since I've started
Briefing you, I would

Like to let you know that
By the end of the judgement
Every single penny in your name, you'll forfeit

That includes your husband's
And, of course, your daughters'
The Acting Governor just signed eight bills

That will make this claim Legal
Unlike you, I operate within the aisle
Of the state's Law. I swear. I'll

Render your lineage broke for eternity
I'm Chief Dan I control ever activity
Of Kaivu. You shouldn't have mustered the audacity

To challenge me. You're just a woman
Not even a Superwoman.
You're no match for a sausage man

Of my calibre. In case
You still have an interest in having sex
With me, I can adjourn the court for weeks."

"I'm not hungry
I'm angry
I'm going crazy

Thanks but no thanks.
I need to address my faithfuls.
My good people, today's

Judgment will be a leap in the right direction
This is the hour of Liberation
If the Judge decides to give the truth no attention

We'll fight, though not with blood, but with our pen
We'll spread the word to mankind. In
No distant time we'll weaken

The shackles of the Wicked
We'll put an end
To these Principalities that has oppressed

Us all. Like I said
Last week, I will decrease and
We all will increase. Today I've decreased

Let us increase this minute
Spread the word to the North
To the South, East and West

I'm not afraid of death
Death's but a cheat
He's afraid that I'll not give up without a fight

This is for the entire state
This is for us all, we the children of fate
This is for us all, that have chosen to fight

Our battles, the Almighty God will fight
God bless our state
God bless Kaivu State."

There was chaos
And hopefully more chaos
Will envelop the Court's Complex

"My Lord, this documentary is a whistleblower story.
It's nothing but the truth. Very
Concise and evidentiary."

The cheaters turned in a documentary
That allegedly
Proved I was guilty

"There's a misunderstanding somewhere."
Truly, God's everywhere
Today he fought our battles fair and square

After the judgement, I laid down my hair
I walked on the air
While the cheats tried vanishing into the thin air

The documentary was about their evil deeds
Not mine. What he wished for me became his
"At last victory's ours..."

—

"Now we're in the State House
Please, Doc I know you've made your points
But people need your services."

Tella gets on my nerves
Every now and then. She knows
My plan. I've had my justice

That's enough. I came to avenge
My family, not to manage
The affairs of a state. I know I utilized a change

Slogan but truth doesn't change
I wouldn't want to derange
The state. I've had my orange

Moment. I rather resign
Into the night than
Drive my faithfuls insane

"All I did, I did for my father
I did for my mother
And for my eternal-year-old brother

My father lost his life snatching
A ballot box for Chief Dan. Dan did nothing
To reward such stupid loyalty. Not a thing.

My pregnant mother kicked the bucket.
My only brother had to meet the world at eight
And worst

He left me forever
Barely a year old. My brother
Died in front of the City's Hospital. My brother

Died in my arms. I'll never
Forget that incident, never.
We were hit by some hit and run driver

We were hawking on the street. I had
Him on my back. Then he pled
For a leak. I laid

My groceries down
And his life he laid down
He would've been

Alive, he could've lived on
But the good for nothing
Hospital was on strike. In

Thirteen months I lost my entire family
Thanks to Dan and his family
Life isn't easy

For a family, talk more of a girl
Of fourteen. For real
I met the worst. I've gone for days without a meal

Not a single meal
Life wasn't gentle
At night I'll kneel and pray and squeal

For Mother of God to descend
From heaven with a plate of food
And a bottle of coke. But she surprised

Me like the others
She didn't show up, not once
Somehow I managed, till I ran out of means.

I'm a troubled soul
Prof. Badmus please tell
Tella that I'm not the real deal."

"Doc isn't the real deal, Tella."
Prof. Badmus' my deputy, you remember
We perfected the plans together

"Tella, Doc isn't a real deal alone. But
With her other half plus us, we'll get
Kaivu up and running, I bet."

It skipped me that I'm married
With three daughters. And I headed
For them, arms widespread

"Mom, we missed you a lot."
"You girls missed me but
I swear I missed you girls the most."

"Don't ask about dad, that
Man's playing hard to get."
I crushed into his arms. Our lips met.

My heel weakens
"A minute, please."
I removed the high heels

Who those two help
We threw away the gap
Between us. Keeping it there's a mishap

"Parental guidance activated.
Girls, we aren't needed
I should get to my wife now I'm all heated."

My deputy exits
Michelle, Grace, and Ivory exits
Tella exits

My day one in that office
Will be memorable, I guess
My dress's getting in the way. He rips

Them in three attempts
Takes my belongings
Between his lips. Like some burnt offering, he lays

Me on the alter. Sorry, the table. Then the files,
Keyboard, monitor on the table jumped off the cliff. Nice
"I'm scared. I'm a virgin. Please

Please...
I haven't done this before. Please."
Nothing turns my husband on like naughty words

In one attempt, he ripped me apart
"Help!" I think I renewed my virginity. I felt
Like it was my first

"Doc, can I be of help. You know, certainly
He can't hurt the two of us easily."
That's Tella. Why's she behind the door. "Silly

Girl, you need a life.
Awww. You need a life
You. You. You. Need a life

—

Behind the Doors
"Why's mom so loud and mad whenever she's having sex
And why's dad so mean and brutal during sex?

I thought lovemaking is another phrase for having sex
Like serious, I see no atom of love in their sex
And if whatever those two are doing inside is sex

I will rather be a Catholic Reverend Sister than have sex."
"Grace, don't be mean on yourself. Sex's solemn and dauntless."
"Michelle's right, it's mom to shout. She is way too serious."

"Ivory, I shout in bed, but your mom's shout tires me."
"Doc tires me. But, my wife's on the calm side.
I do stop from time to time to check if she's still alive."

"Saint Barnabas! How come you all share the same opinion?"
"We've all been there before. It's a fun state to be in."
"Total fun."

"Newsflash. I haven't.
Michelle hasn't.
My junior sister Ivory haven't."

"I have been there several times."
"Age is just a number. Big sister. I've been there, Not once. Not twice."
"How come I'm the only virgin in this house?"

Chapter One - Why Crafters Love SVG Files

When working with your Cricut machine you want to have many files available for your varied projects. Over time you'll build up your own library of favorites. Many Cricut users find SVG's to be the best type of files to use. They are considered a higher quality file for many reasons.

SVG is short for scalable vector graphic (also referred to as a cut file, vector or vectorized image) it's a set of instructions telling the cutter what to do. Think of it like connecting the dots. The cutter needs to follow a path to cut out the design. Unlike PNG or JPG images which are in bitmap form and made up of millions of tiny pixels.

Since a cutting machine cuts using lines and points you can see why using SVG files provide you with a technical advantage and produce superior designs.

The files you buy from Cricut are already SVG files, but if you find images in other formats online you want to use you may choose to convert them to SVG. We discuss how to do this in Chapter Three.

Advantages of using SVG files

The images are easy to use because they are already "clean". You don't have to eliminate a lot of the white background as you would with other types of files. There isn't as much cropping, editing, or erasing required. The checkered background on your screen means the background is erased and that's how a SVG file should appear when you upload it into Design Space.

You simply click on the free file, download it, save it, and then upload. The designer created it with a transparent background which is the advantage of SVG files, they are ready to go. However, you may want to resize or edit in some other way, but you don't have to waste time removing the background to make them usable.

TIP: If you resize a SVG remember to resize proportionately and include all layers so that everything fits together like it was originally designed.

Another advantage is SVG files are scalable. You can enlarge or compress them and they'll maintain high quality resolution unlike a PNG or JPG, which losses quality when resized. A SVG image will stay clear no matter how much you enlarge it.

When the SVG is uploaded it automatically separates into individual layers which make the design process easier. Each layer can be a different color.

Another advantage is that even the free SVG files are completely customizable you can edit them to whatever you desire making them fit any craft project. Add to, flip or rotate the design. Change the color, pattern and size of an element of even hide parts you don't like.

When you upload a PNG or JPG image onto the Cricut Design Space canvas it will ask if you want to save it as a simple, moderately complex, or complex image. With a SVG file you skip this step.

SVG files are usually small which makes them ideal for downloads since they use less space on your hard drive.

All of these benefits make SVG cut files the perfect choice to use with Cricut Design Space.

TIP: The file was created to be cut at a specific size if you reduce the size to much it will be too hard to cut all the tiny details and the quality of the complex design may be lost.

Add tags to organize images

With more than 150 sites to choose from you will soon have tons of SVG's on your hard drive. So how do you find the one with all the cute kittens you downloaded last year? Use tags to describe the image, here's how.

Go to the JPG that came in the downloaded SVG folder. Right click on it and look for Properties, click it. Then click Details. Look for Tags, click it. That will open a box that says Add a tag. Type keywords describing the image separated by a comma. When finished click Ok. Now when you search for files use the keyword to find all the images tagged with it.

There are more organizing suggestions later in the book.